"EVERYBODY LOVES SOMETHING. EVEN IF IT'S JUST TORTILLAS." THE POINT IS TO TOUCH IN TO THE GOOD HEART THAT WE ALREADY HAVE AND NURTURE IT.

~ PEMA CHÖDRÖN

FOR FRANK AND CHARLESTON, MY AWESOME
KIDDOS. YOU HAVE HELPED OPEN MY EYES TO MORE
POSSIBILITIES THAN I'VE EVER IMAGINED... JUST BY
BEING YOU.

FINDING MY AWESOME
Published by Kindness Kids 2021

All inquiries should be directed to
www.MollyMahoney.com

ISBN-13: 978-0-578-94381-7 Paperback
ISBN-13: 978-0-578-94382-4 Hardcover

FINDING MY AWESOME

Confidence, Self-Love, & Joy

BY **MOLLY MAHONEY** &
EEVI JONES

Hi there, I'm Molly. And I'm known to be SUPER duper confident. You know, where I believe in myself and think 'I can' instead of 'I can't!'

But it wasn't always this way! Especially when others around me would say unkind things about my beautiful freckles. That's always when I would start doubting myself...

All that changed after Grandpa shared a humongously, gigantic secret with me. Do you wanna know what that secret is?

Okay! Okay! I knew you'd be curious! You're just like me! That's probably why I like you!

Grandpa told me about this magical *Cloak of Joy*. To make this magical *Cloak of Joy*, I'd have to go on a quest - you know, where you search for stuff.

He calls it his "Quest of Awesome."
There's just ONE rule:

You MUST be
SUPER curious if you
want to play.

Because that's the only way you can make it
through this quest.

Are you SUPER curious? You know, like asking questions, giving new things a try, and being okay to stumble here and there? If you are, I want to hear you say...

YEP! THAT'S ME!

Great! I knew you'd be up for the challenge! Let's do this!

The first step of Grandpa's 'Quest of Awesome' is to get curious and think of something that you're really, REALLY good at. I mean, seriously good!

Want to know the things I'm really, REALLY good at?

I'm REALLY good at touching my nose with my tongue! See, like this! It's not hard at all, but not many people can do it. Can you?

Another thing I'm really, REALLY good at is blowing seriously HUUUGE bubbles with my bubble gum. Have you ever seen a bubble this big?

I love my fun and silly skills. What are yours?

FINDING MY AWESOME

Skills: ✓touching nose with tongue
blowing bubbles

I always write them down. See, just like this! That way, I always remember all the things my awesome self CAN do, and don't worry about those I can't do just yet.

'Cause as Grandpa always loves to say about my seriously mind blowing bubble-blowing skills:

The second step of Grandpa's 'Quest of Awesome' is to get curious and think of something that you really, REALLY love about yourself. I mean, seriously love, like something you would never ever want to trade in a million years, 'cause it's just too special and so YOU.

I absolutely love, love, LOVE my wild, untamable hair.
Isn't it just beautiful? And it's all mine!

Another thing I really, REALLY love about myself are my fun, bright green glasses! Have you ever seen such fun glasses before?

I just LOVE the way I look! What do YOU love about yourself?

FINDING MY AWESOME

skills: ✓touching nose with tongue
blowing bubbles
About me: ✓my wild hair
✓my fun glasses

I used a red marker to write mine down, just in case!
That way, I always remember all the things that are
awesome about me, even when I don't feel like it sometimes.

'Cause as Grandpa always loves to say about my wild, beautifully untamable hair:

"If you love all the things that make up the whole you, it won't ever matter what others say, think, or do!"

The third step in Grandpa's 'Quest of Awesome' is to get curious and think of an activity that you really, REALLY love doing. I mean, seriously love! Like something you want to do over and over and over again - even in your sleep, 'cause it's just so much fun.

I absolutely LOVE taking really bubbly bubble baths with my rainbow bath bombs. They're the best and smell SO good!!!

Another thing I really, REALLY enjoy doing is singing, especially when Grandpa is playing the piano! It doesn't matter what time of day or where I am. If I feel like it, I just start to sing at the top of my lungs. It makes me feel amazing!

These are my most favorite things to do in the whole wide world! What things make you feel amazing?

FINDING MY AWESOME

Skills: ✓touching nose with tongue
blowing bubbles

About me: ✓my wild hair
✓my fun glasses

Activities: bubble bath
singing

Let's write them down, right now! That way, we always remember all the awesome things we get to do, especially when we're feeling sad.

'Cause as Grandpa always loves to say about my top-of-the-lungs singing:

"If you love all the things that make up the whole you, it won't ever matter what others say, think, or do!"

The fourth step of Grandpa's 'Quest of Awesome' is to get curious and think of something that you really, REALLY love and care for. Something that is super-duper important to you, and that you care for SO much that it makes your heart burst, 'cause you just can't imagine a world without it!

I absolutely LOVE my little brother. And I LOVE being KIND to him, even when it's a bit tough sometimes, like when he gets really loud and angry when he can't find his binky...
I know that if I'm kind and show him how much I really love him, he'll feel better because he knows I care.

Something else I really, REALLY love and value are my friendships.

My friends are just the silliest bunch!

They are important to me and make me SO happy!
What are some values that YOU love and bring you joy?

FINDING MY AWESOME

Skills: ✓touching nose with tongue
blowing bubbles
About me: ✓my wild hair
✓my fun glasses
bubble bath
Activities: singing
being kind
Values: ♥my friends

Don't forget to add them to your list! That way, you
always remember that you're never alone, even when
you may feel like it sometimes.

'Caaaause... I'm sure by now you already know what Grandpa always loves to say about having a silly, nilly bunch as your friends:

"If you love all the things that make up the whole you, it won't ever matter what others say, think, or do!"

And finally, the last and fifth step of Grandpa's 'Quest of Awesome' is my favorite one of all! Are you ready for it? 'Cause I sure am!

Now you REALLY have to get curious and think of something that you really, REALLY love... eating. I mean the lick-your-plate-clean kind of love, 'cause you just can't get enough of it!

I absolutely LOVE eating Banana Splits. The combo of ice cream, bananas, chocolate syrup, and whipped cream is the yummiest invention EVER! And don't forget the cherries on top!

Something else I really love eating ALL THE TIME is pasta! Spaghetti, Macaroni, Rigatoni - it doesn't matter what kind! If it's spelled P-A-S-T-A, I'll eat it. Especially with Brussels sprouts on top!

That's what I love to eat the absolute mostest!
What about you?

FINDING MY AWESOME

Skills: ♥touching nose with tongue
blowing bubbles
About me: ♥my wild hair
♥my fun glasses
bubble bath
Activities: singing
being kind
Values: ♥my friends
banana split!!!
Eat: ♥PASTA (+brussels sprouts)

I scribbled mine down already. See? Just like this! That
way, I always remember that my taste buds and
opinions matter, and that we don't always have to agree
with one another.

'Cause as Grandpa always loves to say about my bizarrely terrific taste buds:

Now you may be wondering what in the world this quest has to do with Grandpa's magical *Cloak of Joy*?
I'm glad you asked!

All my answers I found in this quest are super powerful
and magical, because everything on this list
makes me feel happy and joyful! And whenever I'm
happy and joyful, I feel strong and super CONFIDENT
- you know, where I believe in myself and think 'I can'
instead of 'I can't!'

That's why the things come together to make my super magic *Cloak of Joy*. Every time I read through my list, these words jump off the page and wrap themselves around me. It will work for you too!

SMELLY SLUDGE
STINK BUG

TOUCHING NOSE WITH TONGUE
BLOWING BUBBLES
MY FRIENDS
PASTA*BRUSSELS SPROUTS
BANANA SPLIT
BUBBLE BATH
SINGING
WILD HAIR

Nothing breaks through it, not even a bully's unkind words, like *Stink Bug* or *Smelly Sludge*.

See? This negative stuff bounces right off!

So every day, I go through my list of all the things I really, REALLY love, put my hand on my heart, and say out loud - YEP! THAT'S ME! That's when my *Cloak of Joy* activates and magically wraps itself around me.

BEING KIND

TOUCHING NOSE

PASTA

MY FRIENDS

NOSE BANANA SPLIT!

MY FUN GLASSES

WILD HAIR

SINGING

BLOWING BUBBLES

Try it!!! Doesn't this make you feel all warm, fuzzy, and powerful?

And best of all, you can help others find THEIR AWESOME by sharing this quest with them, so they can make their own *Cloak of Joy*.

Got your list? Great! Be sure to look at it often.
It will remind you of all the things that are
really, really **AWESOME** about you!

And remember...

SINGING

JUMPING

"If you love all the things
that make up the whole you,
it won't ever matter what
others say, think, or do!"

MY WILD HAIR

BUBBLE

DANCING

BEING KIND

WHISTLE

MAGIC

PASTA

ABOUT THE AUTHORS

Molly Mahoney "Magical Molly" was born obsessed with Silver Linings. From dancing on tour with a flying car to singing on ships that sailed the world, she knows anything is possible. She now helps business owners to unlock their inner awesome and turn their message into a movement. She loves to #stand4joy from her #pretendcruise with her bass playing husband and kiddos.

You can learn more about Molly at www.ThePreparedPerformer.com

Eevi Jones is a Vietnamese-American *USA Today* and *Wall Street Journal* bestselling writer and award-winning children's book author.

She lives near D.C. with her husband and their two boys.

Eevi can be found at www.BravingTheWorldBooks.com.

OTHER BOOKS BY MOLLY MAHONEY

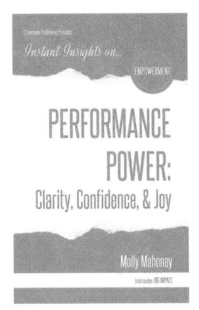

Would you like to walk into any situation and take command with a fearless sense of clear, focused determination? Would you like to present yourself with a contagious, positive energy, leaving others begging for an encore?

You can!

After years of performing in NYC, Las Vegas, Regional Theaters, and on Cruise Ships, Molly Mahoney has taken all she has learned as a performer and reformatted it into a teachable system.

This system will give you the power to attack your goals and wow your clients with clarity, confidence, & joy. This boost of performance power is the perfect polishing touch for connecting with others and making a real impact, from your first impression to every connection you make along the way.

After experiencing a boost of Molly's "performance power," you'll bring a newfound sense of stage presence with you as you take your own "show" on the road.

EVEN MORE FUN

Want video, audio, action sheets, and more to help you find your Awesome and share it with the world?

Go to:

www.FindingMyAwesome.com

We've also included your own *Finding My Awesome* sheet that you can cut out and fill out right away.

And if you make copies of it, you can even share it with your friends! Have so much fun finding your incredible Awesome!!!

FINDING MY AWESOME

Skills:

....

....

....

About me:

....

....

....

Activities:

....

....

....

Values:

....

....

....

Eat:

....

....

....

CPSIA information can be obtained
at www.ICGtesting.com
Printed in the USA
LVHW071106220921
698449LV00002B/8

9 780578 943824